First published in Great Britain in 2007
by Zero To Ten,
Part of Evans Publishing Group
2A Portman Mansions
Chiltern Street, London W1U 6NR

British Library Cataloguing in Publication Data
Clibbon, Meg
Fairyland olympics
1. - Pictorial works - Juvenile literature
I. Title
398.2’454

ISBN 978 1 84089 504 9 (hb)

The Fairyland Olympics

Mighty Meg

would be the first to admit that she lacks sporting talent, despite having several gifted relatives. She is, however, an excellent spectator and is very happy to provide refreshments and encouragement.

Lucy Longlegs

comes from a lengthy line of long-legged sprinters. She likes to kick-start each morning by running through the Enchanted Forest before settling down to a good day's painting!

Dedicated to the sporty Liptrot family

Introduction

One day a very excited wizard on his magical broomstick gatecrashed a meeting of important residents of the Enchanted Forest. They were arguing about what sort of party they should hold in the summer. “Stop!” said the wizard, so they did. “I’ve just come back from the world of humans. They have something called the Olympic games once every four years. It is a sort of great big sporting party. Why don’t we do something like that?”

So they did.

4
3

The Venue

Getting started wasn't easy. The owl architect had to ask the Fairy Queen for permission to build on her land. Health and Safety goblins had to check all the details. And lots of very grumpy local residents needed to be offered lovely new toadstool homes to move out of the way. After the games the guardians of the forest promised to return the land to its original perfect condition.

The owl architect explained his plans and showed how the forest would look during the event.

1. The Misty Mountain

This is for special snow and ice events such as slalom surfing, lightning throwing, glacier gliding and ice dancing.

2. Arboreal Grotto

for the more aesthetic, leafy and musical events.

3. Swamp

for Troll dancing, mud wrestling and Ogre yoga. The muddier the better!

4. Rainbow Podium

for award giving and prizes.

5. Theatair

for aerial events such as cloud gymnastics, sliding down moonbeams, wand waving and air acrobatics.

6. Spherena

This is a great sphere in the middle of the Enchanted Forest, with a flat jousting and tournament area, ideal for all the track events.

7. Sea Palace

This is for the water events and it includes underwater seating around the coral reef.

8. The Games Village

This is the temporary home for all the athletes competing in the games.

OPEN
HERE

5
6
8

Preparations

Giants were in charge of construction.

Deep in the underground kitchens, food fairies and gourmet goblins started cooking.

Mermaids from the Seven Seas Choir swam in to rehearse for the Opening Ceremony.

Cloud Eagles, Silver Swans and the Phoenix donated feathers for winners' coronets.

Volunteers sorted out all the details
needed for such an important event.

Traffic trolls ran the transport.
They were scary but effective.

Air traffic control centres stopped
flying creatures, especially dragons and
wizards, from crashing into each other.

Fairy princesses demanded golden
coaches pulled by unicorns and
accompanied by liveried servants.

Fairy godmothers began
to make banners, bunting
and beautiful decorations.

The Olympic Flag
stars – symbol of aspiration
rainbow – symbol of harmony
waves – symbol of the forces of nature
The Olympic Motto
Fitness, fairness,
fantasy and fun.

The Olympic Oath

I promise to do my best without cheating.
If I win I will be kind to the losers.
If I lose I will be pleased for the winners.
I will accept the decisions of the judges.
I will enjoy taking part.

Invitations

Invitations were sent by Robin Post to competitors throughout the Magic World.

Invitation to attend

We, the Magical Olympics Committee, extend
a warm invitation to all members of the
Magic Empire to come from far and wide
from the depths of the ocean to the highest hill,
from the darkest cavern and the brightest cloud to
gather in the great meeting place of the enchanted
forest where wondrous feats of bravery, skill, speed
and cunning will be tested. Come and be welcome.
Bring family and friends.

RSVP The Wizard of the Woods
Secretary General of the Magical Olympics Committee

Opening Ceremony

The sun is shining on a multi-coloured throng of excited spectators and all the competitors are ready to enter. At last with a flash of lightning the Wizard of the Woods gives a signal and the procession begins. There are flags, banners and special team costumes. The entry of the dragons breathing fire and party poppers is awe-inspiring but the sky-diving by the Red Eagles display team calms everyone down and the sea-horses pulling mermaids through crystal canals are truly beautiful. The crowd is at a fever-pitch of excitement as the opening ceremony draws to a close. The great golden gates open – let the games begin!

A page from the *Magic Mercury* dated the day of the opening ceremony.

Disaster Strikes Magical Olympics
PIRATES INVADE GAMES

a report by our Special Correspondent Sally Sprinter

The opening ceremony of the first Magical Olympics was drawing to its close when a terrifying event occurred. Pirate ships flying the Jolly Roger were spotted sailing up the Crystal Canal towards the centre of the Spherena. Pirates waving cutlasses and hooks lined the decks and threatened to come ashore.

Basil Blackbottom the Pirate
Photos by Flash Lightning

Basil Blackbottom, a spokesman for the pirates declared that they were upset and offended that they had not been invited.

The Wizard of the Woods pointed out to them that they were humans and therefore not qualified to join in, but, after lengthy negotiations, peace was restored when they were allowed to participate in some events, providing that knights were offered an invitation, too. This was agreed and the menacing pirates retreated below decks for grog and biscuits. Mermen escorted the pirate ships to the Sea Palace Centre and the ceremony concluded with a daystar and rainbow light show.

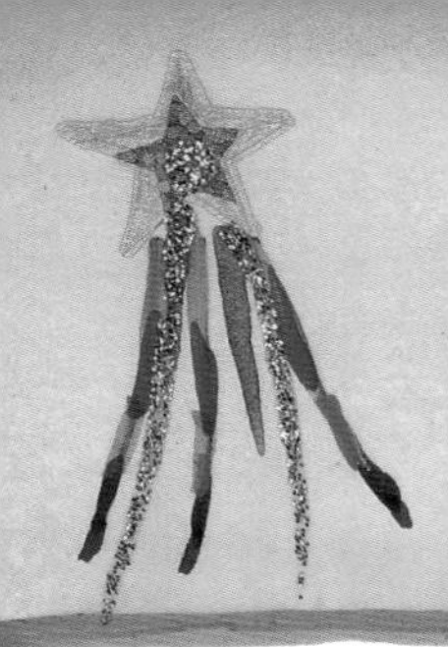

Celebrity Profiles

Scowling Jack walked the plank, swam three times round the lagoon pursued by a crocodile and climbed the mast in ten seconds.

Trug the Traffic Troll was brought into the tree tossing team at the last minute and tossed a pine tree right out of the Spherena.

Fairy Mary broke her wing just before the synchronised flying and still took part in the winning team.

Greta the Goblin went the wrong way in tunnel digging race, made a hole in the lagoon and kept her finger in the hole till help came.

Events

The Games included many spectacular events.

cloud surfing and trapezing

Pegasus cloud jumping

synchronized wand waving

princess dancing

troll tree tossing

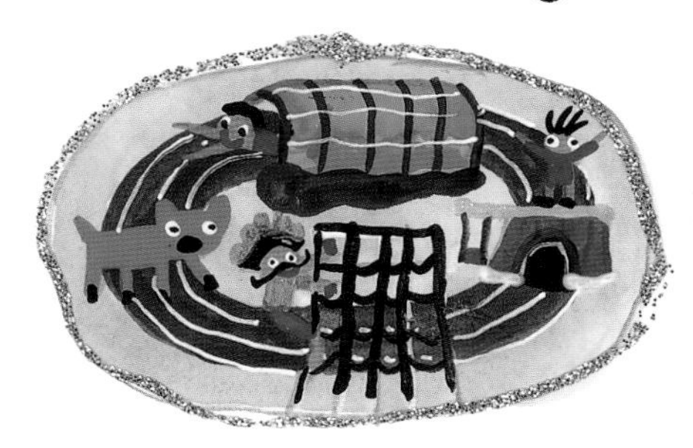

obstacle races

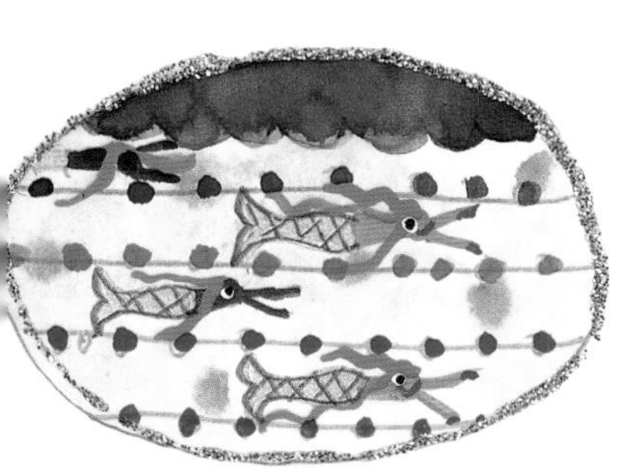

mermaid swimming

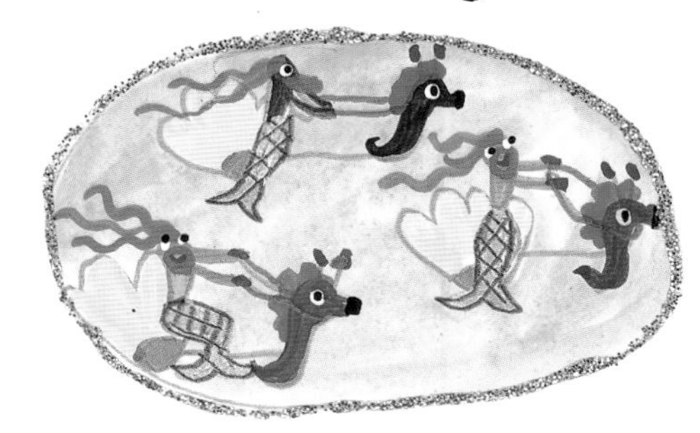

scallop shell chariot racing

trident fighting

The Rainbow Relay

A live report from the Spherena:
Announcer: "Now, over to Gary Gigglebottom, who's down by the finishing line for one of the most anticipated events of the games ... the Rainbow Relay."
Gary: "And here they come, on the last leg of this thrilling race. This huge crowd has been gripped from the start and as they come round the final bend we can see the ogre taking

the baton from the dragon, the fairy passing to the pirate ... but wait ... and here comes Wanda the wizard, from the indigo team, overtaking the violet team's hot favourite Princess Penelope, and sprinting past the pack to win in a scintillating finish! The crowd goes wild! They can't believe it! No one expected the indigo team to set such a magical time, it's like a fairytale dream come true. These underdogs have posted a record that will be hard to beat."

The Theatair

Sun, moon, stars and rainbows illuminate the beautiful theatair where the aerial events take place.

Sliding down
moonbeams
Fairy wand
waving
Dewdrop café

Here is the Games village. (1) Garden with delicious healthy vegetables. (2) Kitchen making lots of food with delicious healthy vegetables. (3) Herb fairies in the cottage hospital looking after people who haven't been eating delicious healthy vegetables, as well as pirates who have been fighting and athletes with strains and aches. (4) Play house and dormitory for baby fairies who sleep in floating beds. Streamers turn

into sparkling lights at bed time. (5) Woven willow arches link the different areas, like the toadstool cottages for athletes – no toadstool comes big enough for giants or smelly enough for ogres so they live elsewhere. (6) Shops selling delicious healthy vegetables, wing shine cream, designer leotards, rosewater sugar lumps for unicorns, fin rings for mermaids and everything else you can imagine.

Each competitor feels the honour of taking part
but there are special prizes for the winners.

In first place

A golden coronet which gives long life and wisdom
(One of the fairy princesses was delighted to win the first prize of long life and everyone else was delighted that she was given wisdom.)

In second place

A silver coronet which gives health and happiness
(One of the trolls won second place in the Underground Obstacle Race and was disgusted to be awarded health and happiness.)

In third place

A bronze coronet which helps you to fly
(Fortunately none of the pirates won third prizes because a flying pirate is something you do not want!)

Health, Fitness and Fun

Winning prizes is wonderful but taking part is the most important thing, no matter who you are, what shape you are, or the age you are.

All the competitors, organisers and spectators agreed that a healthy lifestyle makes everyone a winner. This means eating good food and drinking lots of water and doing plenty of exercise.

Keeping fit can be fun. Fairies exercise their wings every day and elves and pixies do power walking. Swimming is good for mermaids and humans. Even goblins do Morris dancing.

The Closing Ceremony

The final event of the Treetop Marathon brings the games to an end – now it is time for a celebration. It is amazing how many of the competitors who started off by thinking that they were the best now realise that others were better and it doesn't really matter because it was all such fun taking part. The competitors all process around the Spherena with flags, banners and big smiles. The wizard who started it all tosses fireworks and lightning at everyone to create a happy spectacle. Everyone agrees to come back again in four years' time.

Things to Do

Garden Olympics

Organise your own Olympic Games. Make up your own events which are fun but safe. Draw event cards and invitations for your friends. Make special coronets for the winners. Finish the events with a party.

Winners' Coronets

You will need foil paper in 3 colours, preferably gold, silver and bronze. Each coronet should be made like this: 1. Cut a strip of thin card to go round your head with enough for an overlap. 2. Fasten with staples, paper-clips or glue, and decorate with foil shapes (like feathers).

Energy drink

You will need:

1 banana
orange juice
soft fruit such as strawberries

Whizz all the ingredients together in a blender and drink immediately.

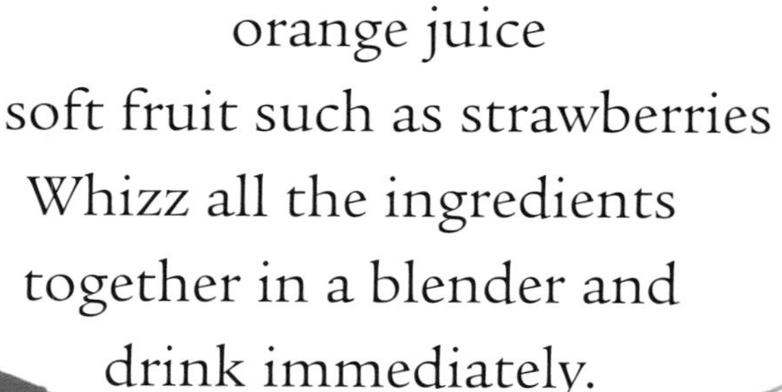